Distributed in Canada by H. B. Fenn and Company Ltd.
Cataloging-in-Publication Data is on file at the Library of Congress
ISBN: 978-1-59643-398-4

Roaring Brook Press books are available for special promotions and premiums.
For details contact: Director of Special Markets, Holtzbrinck Publisher

First Edition May 2010 Book design by Jennifer Browne
Printed in China by RR Donnelley Asia Printing Solutions Ltd., Dongguan City, Guangdong Province
5 7 9 8 6 4

LAURA VACCARO SEEGER

What if?

A NEAL PORTER BOOK

ROARING BROOK PRESS

NEW YORK

What if . . . ?

And what if . . . ?

Then what if . . . ?

But then . . .

Or . . .

What if . . . ?

And what if . . . ?

Then what if . . . ?

But then . . .

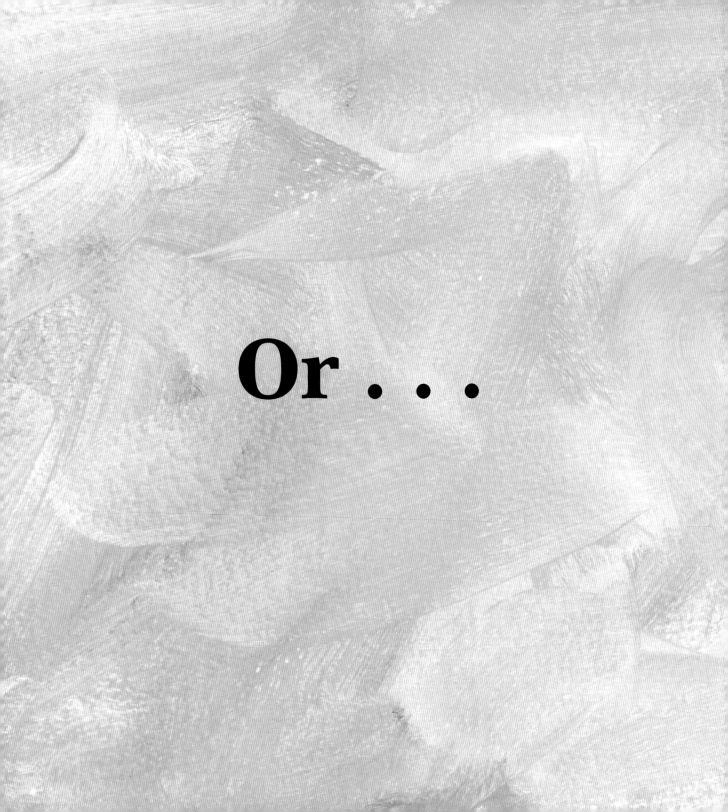

Or . . .

What if . . . ?

And what if . . . ?

Then what if . . . ?

And then . . .